D0326734

A MESSAGE TO PARENTS

It is of vital importance for parents to read good books to young children in order to aid the child's psychological and intellectual development. At the same time as stimulating the child's imagination and awareness of his environment, it creates a positive relationship between parent and child. The child will gradually increase his basic vocabulary and will soon be able to read books alone.

Brown Watson has published this series of books with these aims in mind. By collecting this inexpensive library, parent and child are provided with hours of pleasurable and profitable reading.

©1992 Brown Watson Ltd.
ENGLAND.
Printed in Great Britain

Maurice
The Old Motor Car

Text by Maureen Spurgeon

Brown Watson

ENGLAND

Maurice the motor had once been the smartest car on the road. His headlamps shone, his windows sparkled and his paint-work gleamed.

And whether it was an outing to the seaside or picnics in the summer, parties or trips into town in the winter, everyone was always so pleased to see him.

But when he began getting rusty and his seats started to sag, Maurice was sold to a man who mended motorbikes. He kept what he called his "bits and pieces" on the back seat.

Then came the day when the man bought a brand new van.

"Grandad will be having you, Maurice," he said. "Your gears creak and your engine wheezes, but you won't be going far from now on."

Maurice tried hard not to mind too much. But all too soon, the old man could no longer drive him around, and he was dumped in the corner of a scrap-yard.

Poor Maurice! All he could see were old washing machines, worn-out tyres and every sort of rubbish you can think of. There was nothing to do, nobody to talk to.

Being out in the rain meant he quickly got rustier than ever. Then, his roof started to leak.

"Surely," old Maurice thought, "nobody could hate rain more than me!" But, he was wrong....

Maurice was so miserable, cold and tired, he hardly noticed two little mice paying him a visit. They needed to shelter inside for a very special reason....

The two mice were soon busy, chewing up bits of paper blown in by the wind and tearing strips of rag to weave with some of the loose straw from Maurice's back seat. He didn't mind, at all!

Maurice guessed that something exciting was about to happen, the way the two mice kept chattering and squeaking to each other. He could hardly believe he had so many new friends, all at once!

And the mice were not the only ones who decided to make their home with Maurice. The moment sharp-eyed Mrs. Robin saw the old car, she knew that was where she wanted her nest.

With a family of robins singing so sweetly all day and the lively mice scampering around and playing in their nice little home, Maurice decided he had never been happier!

Then, one morning, everything changed. No birds sang, no mice squeaked and chattered. Surely, Maurice told himself, his friends would not have left him so suddenly? But, they had.

Maurice felt so sad. He was still trying to think what could have happened, when he heard a tiny cry coming from the front seat. It sounded just like a tiny kitten, mewing!

"So that's why the mice and the robins left so suddenly," smiled Maurice to himself, knowing how frightened they would be with a cat around.

As for her kittens, it was plain they loved being with Maurice. When they were not playing together outside, he could hear them purring as they slept underneath the steering wheel.

The only thing that worried him was the thought of the kittens growing up. Would they leave him then, he wondered? Already they were wandering further and further away – Mother Cat, as well.....

The family to which Maurice had once belonged now seemed so far away, it was quite a shock to hear footsteps and a voice calling out: "Hey, come here everybody! See who I've found!"

"It's Tabitha!" cried a little girl. Maurice could see her stroking the Mother Cat's head.

"We told you we'd seen her near here, didn't we, Daddy? Robert was sure she'd had her kittens."

"And I was right!" shouted her brother, climbing into Maurice's driving seat. "Lucky she found this old car! Isn't it great, Amy?" "Honk—honk!" Amy was much too busy, sounding the horn. "Honk—honk!"

Robert and Amy played for a long time with Maurice. He could tell they did not really want to go home, not even when their Daddy called: "Come along, you two! Tabitha's new family is waiting!"

"We wouldn't mind having the car too!" Maurice heard Robert saying. His Daddy laughed - but what was said next, Maurice didn't know. By the next day, he was so sad, he hardly cared what happened to him.

"Here's the old banger!" said a voice, breaking into Maurice's thoughts. "Engine and gear-box out, right?" "Right!" came the reply. "Must be a spare parts job, I reckon."

"Spare parts!" echoed Maurice. "Don't say I'm to be broken up!" But when his tyres were levered off one by one, and a crane hauled him high into the air, he knew it must be true.

Maurice shut his eyes tight. It seemed nobody wanted him any more. But, when he opened them again what do you think? There were cheers from the back seat!